Valentine's Day Disaster

2nd Grade!

by ABBY KLEIN

illustrated by
JOHN McKINLEY

Scholastic Inc.

To My Family,
Thank you for all of your love and support
throughout this incredible journey!
I couldn't have done it without you!
xo,
A.K.

ISBN 978-1-338-28136-1

10 9 8 7 6 5 4 3   19 20 21 22 23

Printed in the U.S.A.   40

First printing 2019

CHAPTERS

I have a problem. A really, really big problem. Valentine's Day is one of my favorite days of the year, but this year it is turning into a real disaster! Everything is going wrong. Let me tell you about it.

CHAPTER 1

Party Planning

"Tomorrow is a very special day," said our teacher, Miss Clark.

Chloe jumped out of her seat and started twirling around the classroom. "I know what tomorrow is!" she sang. "I know what tomorrow is! La-la-la . . . la-la . . . la!"

"So does everybody else! Ding-da-ding . . . da-ding . . . dong!" Max sang, imitating Chloe's singsong voice.

Chloe tried to ignore him and continued twirling and singing, "Candy and flowers . . . hearts and kisses!"

Max popped up, puckered up his lips, and made kissing sounds with his mouth. "KISS, KISS, KISS, KISS! What are you kissing, monkeys?"

Chloe accidentally bumped into him and went flying to the ground.

"OWWWW!! OWWWW!" she cried. "Miss Clark, Max just pushed me!"

"I did not!" yelled Max. "You bumped into me when you were doing your stupid dancing."

"My dancing is not stupid! I am a ballerina!" Chloe wailed from her spot on the floor.

Jessie rolled her eyes and whispered to me, "There is always craziness with those two."

I laughed.

"I'm confused," said Josh. "Why did she scream 'OWWWW!'? Is she hurt? She doesn't look hurt."

"She's not hurt," Jessie said quietly. "She is such a drama queen. She just loves attention."

"You can say that again," I mumbled.

Miss Clark walked over to Chloe and reached out her hand. "I think you're okay, Chloe. Here, take my hand, and I'll help you up."

"She doesn't need any help," said Max. "She's not really hurt. She's just pretending."

"I am not pretending!" Chloe whined.

"Oh yes you are!"

"Oh no I'm not!"

"Yes you are!"

Miss Clark turned to Max and pointed to his chair. "Sit down now! And don't say another word unless you'd like to go have a little chat with Mr. Pendergast in his office."

Max opened his mouth and was about to say something, but then changed his mind and sat down. I guess he decided he had already been to the principal's office enough times this week.

"Chloe, I can see that you are fine," said Miss Clark. "You are not hurt. Grab my hand and stand up, please."

Chloe took hold of Miss Clark's hand and stood up.

"Great! Now please show me that you can calmly walk back to your seat," said Miss Clark.

Chloe made a point of slowly limping back to her chair.

"See? What did I tell you?" said Jessie. "Drama queen!"

I shook my head and laughed.

Miss Clark walked back to the front of the room. "Now, where were we? With all that commotion, I forgot what I was going to say."

Jessie raised her hand. "You were saying that tomorrow is a special day."

"Oh, that's right. Thanks, Jessie. Yes, tomorrow is Valentine's Day."

"I love Valentine's Day!" Chloe squealed. "It's my favorite day of the year!"

Miss Clark sighed. "Yes, Chloe. We know. Anyway, tomorrow we are going to pass out our valentines and have a party."

"Do we have to bring valentines for *everyone*?" Max blurted out. "What if there are people we don't want to give valentines to?"

"Gee," I whispered to Jessie. "I wonder who he's talking about."

Chloe glared at Max from across the room.

"You don't have to bring in any valentines," said Miss Clark, "but if you do bring them in, then you have to make sure you have one for every person in the class."

"But . . . but . . . ," Max started to protest.

"Those are the rules, Max," said Miss Clark. "We don't want anyone to be left out and have their feelings hurt."

"Whatever," Max grumbled.

I raised my hand.

Miss Clark looked at me and smiled. "Yes, Freddy, did you have a question? Thank you for raising your hand and not just shouting out."

"Did you say we are going to have a party?" I asked.

"Yes, I did," said Miss Clark. "I thought people could bring in treats, and we could play some special games . . ."

"Really?" said Jessie.

Miss Clark nodded and smiled. "Yes, does that sound like fun?"

"That sounds awesome!" said Josh.

"I don't think I've ever played any valentine games before," said Jessie. "I can't wait!"

"Oh! I have a great idea!" Chloe said, jumping up and down.

"Wow!" Josh whispered. "Her leg really healed quickly."

Jessie giggled.

"My nana makes these really cute red hearts out of Jell-O," said Chloe. "Can I bring those in?"

"Sure," said Miss Clark. "Let me write that down on my list."

"Freddy, your mom makes the best sugar cookies," said Josh. "Why don't you bring those in?"

I smiled and gave Josh a thumbs-up. "Great idea! You can come over after school and help me make them."

When Miss Clark looked up from her list, I said, "Josh and I will bring in cookies for the party."

"Cookies! Cookies! I love cookies," Max said, rubbing his belly.

"He sounds like the Cookie Monster," Josh whispered. "Me want cookies! Me want cookies!"

"You crack me up," I said, laughing.

"We'd better make sure we keep those away from Max until the party," said Josh "or there might not be any left."

"My *abuela*, my grandma, makes really good *agua fresca*," said Jessie.

"What's that?" said Max. "I've never heard of it."

"It's from Mexico, and it's really delicious,"

said Jessie. "You mix water, a little bit of sugar, and fruit in a blender."

"I've had that before in California," said Josh. "It *is* really delicious."

"I'll ask my *abuela* to make *agua fresca* with watermelon, then it will be red for Valentine's Day."

Miss Clark added that to her list. "I can't wait to try it, Jessie. It's always fun to try something new. I think we are all set with the treats. Thank you all for volunteering to bring those in. I will plan the games."

Chloe clapped her hands and bounced up and down in her chair. "This is going to be so much fun!"

"I wish it were tomorrow already!" said Jessie.

"Miss Clark, you are the best teacher ever!" I said.

"Why, thank you, Freddy. Thank you so much. What a sweet thing to say."

I blushed, and my cheeks turned the color of Valentine's Day . . . bright red!

CHAPTER 2

Perfect Hearts

"There is one more thing we all have to do before tomorrow," said Miss Clark.

"I know! I know!" Chloe interrupted. "Make valentines! Mine are going to be amazing. I'm making them myself, and they are going to have flowers and pink ribbons, and I'm even going to spray them with a little perfume!"

"Perfume! Yuck!" Max said, holding his nose. "I don't want an eewy, pewy, stinky, rinky valentine!"

"They are not stinky!" Chloe huffed.

11

"Here we go again . . . ," I whispered to Josh and Jessie.

But just as Max opened his mouth, Miss Clark cut him off. "I wasn't talking about making valentines," she said. "You all are doing that at home. I was talking about something else we have to do here at school before our Valentine's Day party tomorrow."

Jessie raised her hand. "I think I know what it is," she said.

Miss Clark smiled. "You do? Tell us what you think this really important job is."

"We have to make something to put all of our valentines in," said Jessie, "so we don't lose them."

"Oh, mine is going to have to be really big," Chloe said, stretching her arms out wide, "because I'm going to get so many valentines!"

"Hey, Fancypants, you're going to have the same number of valentines as everybody else," said Max.

Miss Clark just shook her head and kept talking. "You are right, Jessie," she said, holding up some plain white bags.

"Is that what we are going to put our valentines in?" asked Chloe. "Those are so boring."

"Right now they do look very plain," said Miss Clark. "But your job is going to be to decorate them."

"Cool," said Josh. "That sounds like fun."

"You can decorate them however you want," said Miss Clark. "I have stickers, and construction paper, and glitter, and markers . . ."

"Ooooooo!" said Chloe, clapping her hands with excitement. "I love glitter!"

"Of course she does," whispered Josh. "If it's shiny and sparkly, then she loves it."

"Jessie, will you help me pass out the bags?" asked Miss Clark.

"AWWWW!" Chloe whined. "Why does she get to do it? That's not fair." She put her hands on her hips, stuck out her lower lip, and pouted.

"It's very fair," said Miss Clark. "She has been a good listener all morning and has not interrupted me once."

"Hmph!" Chloe huffed, and stuck out her lower lip even farther.

Jessie passed out the bags, and Miss Clark spread all of the other supplies out on the tables.

Everybody got to work. Everybody except me. I stared at my bag and frowned.

"What's wrong?" asked Jessie. "Why aren't you getting started?"

I let out a big sigh. "I have no idea what to do," I said.

"Seriously?" said Jessie. "What is your favorite thing in the whole wide world?"

"Uh, duh," said Josh. "I think we all know what Freddy's favorite thing is . . . sharks!"

I laughed. "But what do sharks have to do with Valentine's Day?"

"Oh! I know!" said Jessie. "I have a great idea! Why don't you make the shark fins out of upside-down hearts, and you can fill in the body of the shark with silver glitter."

"I love that idea!" I said. "But there's only one problem."

"What's that?" asked Jessie.

"I'm not really good at making hearts. Every time I try to cut one out, it always comes out crooked."

"I know how to make perfect hearts," Chloe boasted, holding up a heart she had just cut out. "It's easy!"

"Of course you do," I mumbled.

"She thinks she's perfect at everything," Josh whispered to me. "Just ignore her."

"I'll show you a trick I know," said Jessie, "so that your hearts come out more even on both sides."

"Okay," I said.

"First, you take a piece of paper like this and fold it in half," said Jessie.

I grabbed a piece of red paper and folded it in half.

"Then you draw half of a heart shape like this, starting from the folded side," Jessie continued.

I picked up a pencil and copied exactly what Jessie just did.

"Great, Freddy! Now keep the paper folded and cut on your pencil line like this," said Jessie.

I cut carefully on my pencil line.

"Now," said Jessie, "open it up and TA-DA! . . . You have a perfect heart!"

I slowly opened up the paper and looked at it. Then I smiled. "Hey, Jessie, look at my heart. It isn't crooked."

Jessie grinned. "I told you it was a good trick."

I turned the heart over in my hand. "It really is perfect." We high-fived each other.

"You just need to cut a few more for the other shark fins," said Jessie.

I got to work cutting out some more hearts using Jessie's trick. They all came out perfect! No more crooked hearts for me.

"Hey, you definitely got the hang of it," said Jessie.

"Yeah," I said. "Now I just need to make the shark's body on my bag." I grabbed a gray marker and drew the outline of the shark.

"You are really good at drawing sharks," said Josh.

"Thanks," I said, laughing. "I've had a lot of practice."

"Are you going to fill in the body with glitter?" asked Jessie.

"Yep," I said. "Where is the glitter?"

"Let me guess," said Jessie. "I bet Little Miss Sparkles has it."

I looked over and sure enough, Chloe was shaking glitter all over everything.

"Hey!" Max barked. "Stop hogging the glitter!" He lunged toward Chloe and tried to yank the bottle out of her hand.

The top of the bottle popped off and glitter flew everywhere. It looked like it was raining glitter.

"Now look what happened, you big meanie!" Chloe cried.

Miss Clark came running over. "Just look at this mess! Max, you need to get a sponge and clean all of this up right now."

Max grunted and shuffled over to the sink.

"Can I have the glitter back?" asked Chloe. "I wasn't done using it yet."

"I think you've used plenty," said Miss Clark. "It's someone else's turn now."

"May I please have it?" I asked.

"Of course, Freddy," said Miss Clark, handing it to me.

I spread some glue on my bag and sprinkled glitter on my shark's body. Then I added the hearts I had cut out as fins. Finally, I drew an eye and a bunch of upside-down hearts as teeth. I held up my bag. "TA-DA!"

"Wow!" said Josh. "That looks awesome, dude."

"It came out perfect," said Jessie.

I smiled. "Yes, it did . . . All because of you. Thanks for the help."

Jessie smiled back. "That's what friends are for."

CHAPTER 3

Crazy Hearts

When the bus pulled up in front of my house, Josh and I jumped off and ran inside.

"Mom! Mom!" I called. "Where are you?"

"I'm in here, Freddy!" she yelled from the kitchen.

We dashed into the kitchen and dropped our backpacks on the floor.

"Oh, hi, Josh. I didn't know you were here," said my mom.

"Hi, Mrs. Thresher," said Josh. "I hope it's okay."

"Of course it's okay," said my mom. "Freddy's friends are always welcome here."

"Guess what, Mom?" I said, bouncing up and down.

"What, honey? It must be something very exciting or else you've got ants in your pants."

"Tomorrow we are not just going to pass out our valentines, but we are also going to have a Valentine's Day party in our class!"

"A party? Really? How fun!" said my mom.

"With games and treats," said Josh.

"Fun *and* yummy," my mom added.

"I volunteered to bring in cookies for the party," I said.

"You did?" said my mom, sounding a bit confused.

"I kind of gave Freddy the idea, Mrs. Thresher," said Josh, "because I think you make the best sugar cookies in the whole wide world!"

"Why, thank you, Josh. That's very sweet of you to say."

Now it was Josh's turn to blush. He turned bright red!

"So can you help me and Josh make heart-shaped cookies for our party tomorrow?" I asked.

"With red frosting," Josh added.

My mom chuckled. "Sure, I can help you make heart cookies with red frosting."

"Woo-hoo!" I said, pumping my fist in the air. "What do we need to do first?" I started walking over to the cupboards.

My mom grabbed the back of my shirt. "Hold on there a minute. The first thing you need to do is wash your hands."

I looked at the back of my hands, and then I turned them over and studied the front. "They look okay to me," I said.

"I don't even want to think about what those hands have touched today," said my mom. She pointed to a brown spot on my palm. "What's that?"

I looked at the spot and shrugged my shoulders. "I dunno," I said. Then I spit into my palm and started rubbing the spot with my finger.

"Freddy, what are you doing?" exclaimed my mom.

"What does it look like I'm doing? Cleaning that spot off my hand."

Josh started laughing. "Dude, that's gross," he said.

"Yes," said my mom. "Very gross! You're not cleaning anything. You're just spreading germs. If you want to bake cookies, then you have to go to the sink and really wash your hands with water, not spit."

"Fine," I grumbled.

"And soap," said my mom.

Josh and I went over to the sink and scrubbed our hands. "All set!" I said as I started to open the refrigerator to get out the eggs.

"Hold on just a minute," said my mom. "I need to inspect those hands." She looked closely at the fronts and backs of our hands.

"Do they pass inspection, sir?" I said, saluting my mom.

My mom laughed. "Yes, they do. Good job."

"What else do we need besides sugar and eggs?" I asked.

"We definitely need flour," said my mom. "I finished up a bag of flour the last time I made cookies, so we have to open a new one."

"I'll get it!" I said. I went to the pantry, picked up the new bag of flour, and brought it over to the counter.

"Do you want me to help you open it?" asked my mom.

"Nope! I got it," I said as I grabbed the sides of the bag in my hands and started to pull.

I guess I pulled a little too hard because the bag ripped wide open and sent a snowstorm of flour flying through the air.

I looked over at Josh and started laughing. "Ha, ha, ha, ha, ha!"

"What's so funny?" said Josh.

"You are!" I said, continuing to laugh

hysterically. "You should see yourself. You look like an old grandpa. Your hair is all white!"

"Well, you should see *yourself*," said Josh. "You are covered in flour. You look like the abominable snowman!"

"Oh my goodness!" said my mom. "Hold still, both of you. I need to get a rag to dust you two off."

We stood like statues until my mom came back and wiped us down with a rag. "There . . . much better," she said.

"Sorry, Mom," I said. "That was an accident. I guess I just pulled a little bit too hard."

My mom smiled, shook her head, and mumbled, "Freddy, Freddy, Freddy. I never know what to expect when you're around."

"It's an adventure," I said, grinning.

"It sure is," said my mom. "Now, let's see . . . We need to crack two eggs into this bowl to start. You each can crack an egg."

"I'll go first," said Josh. He gently picked up an egg, tapped it lightly on the side of the bowl, and cracked it open. The egg slid into the bowl.

"You're like a master chef," said my mom.

"Thanks. My dad taught me how to do that because we make scrambled eggs together every Saturday morning."

"Okay, my turn now," I said. I picked up the second egg and thought I tapped it lightly, just like Josh, but the whole egg cracked in my hand. Yolk was oozing through my fingers and dripping onto my pants, and a bunch of shell pieces fell in the bowl.

"Oops," I whispered. "I guess I don't know how strong I am."

My mom and Josh just started laughing.

"Dude, you are like a walking disaster," said Josh.

"You can say that again," my mom said, chuckling. "It looks like I need another rag."

After she cleaned me up for a second time, Josh and I took turns adding the other ingredients into the bowl and mixing up the dough.

Luckily, there were no other major cooking accidents.

"Now we need to use this rolling pin to roll out the dough. Then we can cut out heart shapes with the cookie cutters." My mom turned to me. "Want to give it a try, Strong Man?"

I lifted up my arms and flexed my muscles.

"Whoa! Watch out!" Josh said, laughing. "Here's comes the next WWF fighter . . . The SHARK!"

I grabbed the rolling pin and pretended to lift it above my head like a strong man with a heavy weight. I even added the grunting sounds like the wrestlers do.

Josh and my mom burst out laughing. "HA, HA, HA, HA, HA!"

We took turns rolling out the dough and cutting the heart shapes. Josh's hearts looked perfect. Mine came out lopsided. I held one up. "It looks like someone sat on this heart," I said. "It's smushed on one side."

"I love it just the way it is," said my mom.

While the cookies were baking, we mixed some red food coloring into the white frosting. I stuck my finger in the frosting and dabbed it on the end of my nose. Then I jumped up on a chair and started singing, "Rudolph the Red-Nosed Reindeer . . ."

My mom covered her face with her hands and giggled.

Josh laughed and said, "You're crazy. You know that, Freddy? Really crazy!"

CHAPTER 4

You Are Jaw-some!

Josh and I finished decorating the cookies, so he went home to work on his valentines. My mom and I were starting to clean up the kitchen when my sister, Suzie, came in from her dance class.

She sniffed the air. "Mmmmmm, it smells amazing in here. I would know that smell anywhere . . . Mom's sugar cookies!"

Then she walked over to the platter of cookies, picked one up, and was about to take a bite when I lunged toward her yelling, "NOOOOOOOO!"

Suzie froze. My body collided with hers and knocked the cookie out of her hand. I leaped up to save it, but it was just out of my reach. The cookie hit the ground and smashed into pieces.

I glared at Suzie. "Look what you did!" I screamed.

"Correction," said Suzie. "Look what *you* did. All I was doing was eating a cookie. I'm not sure why you're freaking out. I was just going to eat one cookie. Besides, they're not even *your* cookies."

"Actually, they *are* my cookies," I said.

"Oh, really?" said Suzie. "Last time I checked, when Mom makes cookies, she makes them for both of us."

"They are *my* cookies for *my* class party tomorrow," I said. "And now I might not have enough for everyone, thanks to you!" I buried my head in my hands.

"Is he about to cry over a cookie?" asked Suzie.

"I'm not crying!" I yelled.

"Freddy, calm down," said my mom. "Suzie didn't do anything wrong. She had no idea these cookies were for your class."

"But now I won't have one for everybody in the class!" I sniffed. "This is a disaster!"

"Don't worry," said my mom. "It's not a disaster. I made some extras just to be safe."

"You did?" I threw my arms around my mom's neck and gave her a big hug. "Thanks, Mom."

Then I turned to Suzie and said, "So now that

you know they're mine, keep your grabby little hands off of them."

"Freddy," said my mom, "that was not a very nice way to speak to your sister. Please try that again."

I stared at the ground.

"Freddy, if you can't talk nicely to your sister, then we won't be able to work on your valentines for tomorrow," my mom continued.

Suzie tapped her foot. "I'm waiting," she said.

I slowly lifted my head and blew out a big breath. "Please don't eat any of those cookies. They are for my class party tomorrow."

"Much better. Thank you," said my mom.

"Hey, speaking of disasters," said Suzie. "What happened in here? It looks like it was hit by a hurricane of flour."

My mom chuckled. "That would be Hurricane Freddy," she said.

"When I opened the bag of flour, it kind of exploded."

"You can say that again," Suzie said, laughing.

"Why don't the two of you get the broom and dustpan and sweep this up while I finish wiping down the counters," said my mom.

"I'll sweep," said Suzie. "You can hold the dustpan."

"Whatever you say, Bossypants," I muttered under my breath.

Suzie whipped her head around. "What did you just say?"

I smiled and fluttered my eyelashes at her. "Whatever you say, sis," I said sweetly.

We finally got the kitchen cleaned up, so we could start working on our valentines. We sat down at the kitchen table, and my mom got out all of the art supplies.

"I know exactly what I'm going to make this year!" Suzie exclaimed, clapping her hands.

Of course she did.

"I saw it online, and it's super cute."

"What is it?" I asked.

"You make these little bees with heart wings, heart eyes, and heart antennae, and then you write 'Bee Mine' on it," Suzie said.

"That does sound really cute," said my mom.

Suzie got right to work like a busy little bee. I just sat there staring at the table.

"Freddy, what's wrong?" asked my mom. "Why aren't you making any valentines? You told me you need them for your party tomorrow."

"UGGHHH!" I groaned. "I have no idea what to make!"

"What do you mean you have no idea?" said Suzie. "You're going to make sharks. That's what you do every year . . . You make sharks because you are obsessed with them!"

"I'm not obsessed with them," I said. "I just really like them."

Suzie shook her head. "Same difference," she mumbled.

My mom tapped her chin with her finger. "Hmmmm . . . Let's see . . . ," she said. "What could you make?"

"When I was looking online, I did see this one cool shark idea," said Suzie.

"You did?" I said. "What did it look like?"

"It looked like that famous shark head. You know, the one from the movie poster for *Jaws*," said Suzie.

"Oh, I love that poster!" I said. "That does sound cool."

"So you cut out a big heart," Suzie continued. "Then you glue on a picture of that shark head, and write 'You are Jaw-some!' on the valentine."

"I love that idea!" I said. I jumped up out of my seat and gave Suzie a big hug. "Thanks, Suzie! You're the best!"

My mom smiled. "Now, Freddy, would you like me to cut out the big hearts for you like I did last year?" my mom asked.

"No thanks, Mom," I said. "Today at school Jessie taught me how to cut out the perfect heart. Watch, I'll show you."

I picked up a piece of red paper, folded it in half, drew half a heart on the fold, and cut it out. I held it up. "TA-DA! A perfect heart!"

"Very nice," said my mom. "That looks great! Jessie is a good teacher. You can cut out your own hearts this year, but you'd better get started because you have to make twenty valentines."

I got right to work cutting out the hearts. Then I went online, printed images of the *Jaws* shark head in color, and glued them onto the hearts. Finally, I wrote "You are Jaw-some" on each one.

I sat back in my chair, crossed my arms over my chest, and let out a great big sigh. "Phew! That was a lot of work!"

"Yes, it was!" said my mom. "And now you are finished."

"Not yet," I said.

"What do you mean 'not yet'? You made twenty, didn't you?"

I nodded. "But I have one more to make."

"You do?" said my mom. "For who?"

I didn't answer.

"I know who it's for," Suzie said. "It's for his girlfriend."

"I don't have a girlfriend!" I shouted at Suzie.

"Geez . . . calm down," said Suzie. "I was just joking."

"Then who is it for?" my mom asked again.

"It's a secret," I mumbled.

"What did you say, Freddy? I didn't hear you," said my mom.

"It's a secret," I said a little louder.

"Oh!" said my mom. "Do you need me to print out one more shark for your secret valentine?"

"No thanks, Mom," I said, and smiled. "This valentine is going to be different. This valentine is going to be extra special."

Suzie looked over at me and raised her eyebrows.

CHAPTER 5

Extra-Special
Valentine

The extra-special secret valentine was going to be for Miss Clark, and I wanted it to be perfect. I also didn't want my mom and Suzie to see it.

"Ummmm . . . Can I bring some art supplies up to my room?" I asked.

"Why?" asked my mom.

"Because I want to work on my last valentine in private," I said.

Suzie poked me with her finger. "See! What did I tell you? It's for his girlfriend."

I swatted her finger away with my hand. "Get your hands off me! And for the last time, it's not for my girlfriend!" I cried. "I don't even have a girlfriend!"

"Whatever you say," Suzie mumbled.

"Suzie," said my mom, "leave Freddy alone. If he doesn't want us to see the valentine he's making, that's fine."

"So can I take some stuff upstairs?" I asked again.

"I don't see why not," said my mom. "Just be careful and don't get any glue on the carpet."

My mom is such a neat freak, so I know she'll be coming up to check if I got any glue on the carpet. "I promise I'll be careful, Mom."

"You don't have a lot of time," my mom added. "Dad will be home soon, and he'll be hungry for dinner."

My stomach grumbled. "Ha! I think that's my stomach asking what's for dinner," I said, laughing.

"I'm not sure," said my mom. "I've spent the whole afternoon baking cookies and making valentines. I haven't had time to think about dinner."

"That means we get to order in pizza! Woo-hoo!" I said, pumping my fist in the air.

"I guess we can do that," said my mom. "What kind of pizza do you guys want?"

"Cheese, cheese, cheesy, cheese!" I sang, and did a little dance.

"What are you doing, dork?" said Suzie.

"I'm doing my pizza dance."

"Do you love pizza?" Suzie asked.

"That's a dumb question," I said. "You know I love pizza."

"Do you love it so much that you want to marry it?" Suzie said, smirking. "Maybe you want to give it a secret valentine . . . huh? Do you?"

"Mom!" I wailed. "Suzie is teasing me. Tell her to leave me alone!"

"Suzie, leave Freddy alone. What kind of pizza do you want?"

"Mushroom," said Suzie.

"EEEWWWW!" I said, scrunching up my nose. "Mushrooms are disgusting. They are slimy and gross. I do *not* want them on my pizza."

"They're not gross," said Suzie. "They are delicious, and *I* want them on my pizza."

"Too bad for you," I said, "because we're getting cheese."

Suzie put her hands on her hips. "Guess what? You don't get to decide," she said. "We're getting mushroom."

I put my nose right in Suzie's face. "Cheese!" I barked.

"Mushroom!" Suzie barked back.

My mom stuck her arms in between the two of us. "All right! That's enough, you two. There is no need to argue. We can get half cheese and half mushroom."

I crossed my arms. "Fine. Just make sure no mushrooms sneak onto my slices of cheese," I said.

My mom laughed. "Mushrooms don't have legs," she said. "I don't think they'll be doing any sneaking around. Now, if you want to make that last valentine, then you'd better get going."

"Oh, right!" I said. I scooped up some of the art supplies and started to walk out of the kitchen.

As I got close to the stairs, I thought I heard something behind me. I turned around just in time to see Suzie duck behind the couch.

I tiptoed over to the couch and peeked over the back. "Gotcha!" I said, grabbing Suzie's shirt. "I knew you were hiding back here. Now stop following me!"

"Let go of my shirt!" she cried.

"Only if you promise not to spy on me," I said.

"Fine. I promise," said Suzie. "Now let me go!"

I let go of her shirt and dashed upstairs to my room. I was running out of time. My dad was going to be home really soon.

As soon as I was in my room, I shut the door. I did not want Suzie spying on me.

I sat down on the edge of my bed and hit my forehead with the palm of my hand. "Think, think, think," I muttered. "What does Miss Clark like?"

I sat there for a moment, and then a great idea popped into my head. "Flowers! Miss Clark loves flowers! I'll make her a valentine with lots of flowers on it."

I sat down on the floor of my room and started cutting out flowers from colored paper.

I know! I thought to myself. *I can make it look like a hand holding a bouquet of flowers.*

I cut out a big heart. *Perfect,* I thought. *Jessie really did teach me how to make perfect hearts!*

Then I traced my hand and cut it out. Finally, I glued the flowers onto the heart, and I glued the hand holding the stems.

I held up the valentine and smiled. *I think Miss Clark will really like this,* I thought.

Just then another great idea popped into my

head. I remembered what Chloe said earlier in class. Perfume! I could spray the valentine with a little perfume to make it extra special. I just had to sneak into my mom's bathroom and borrow a little bit of her perfume.

I slowly opened my bedroom door. I looked to the right and then to the left. The coast was clear, so I tiptoed down the hall into my parents' bathroom. I picked up my mom's perfume bottle and did one quick spray on my valentine. I was just putting the perfume back on the counter when a voice behind me said, "Hey!"

I was so startled that I jumped about six feet in the air and dropped the perfume and the valentine.

"Gotcha!" said Suzie. "What are you doing sneaking around in here?"

I quickly picked up the perfume and the valentine and hid them behind my back.

"You promised you weren't going to spy on me," I said.

"I wasn't spying. Mom sent me upstairs to

tell you that the pizza is here." Suzie tried to look behind me. "Is that Mom's perfume?"

I just stared at her and didn't say a word.

"Ooooo, you are in so much trouble," she said, and started to walk out of the bathroom. "Just wait until I tell Mom what you did."

I grabbed her arm. "Wait! Please don't tell her," I begged.

Suzie grinned. "What's it worth to you?" she said, holding up her pinkie for a pinkie swear.

"Ummm . . . ummm . . . How about a piece of my valentine candy?" I said.

"A piece! Are you kidding? Four pieces or no deal," said Suzie.

"Four pieces!" I said. "That's not fair."

"Take it or leave it," Suzie said, holding up her pinkie one more time. "And I don't have all day. The pizza is getting cold."

"Fine," I grumbled as we locked pinkies. "We have a deal."

CHAPTER 6

Valentine's Day

RIIINNNGGG! RIIINNNGGG! My alarm clock screamed in my ear. I was about to roll over and hit the snooze button when I remembered it was Valentine's Day. I leaped out of bed and ran to the bathroom.

The door was closed, so I pounded on it. "Hey! Open the door!" I yelled. "I need to get in there. It's an emergency!"

"You can wait, Sharkbreath!" Suzie said.

"But I have to brush my teeth," I whined.

"That's not an emergency," she answered through the door. "You can do that after you get dressed. Besides, brushing your teeth doesn't really help with that stinky shark breath of yours."

"You are such a pain!" I shouted.

I ran back into my room and yanked open my dresser drawer. I started digging through my shirts to find my red shark shirt to wear today.

"Ah-ha! Here it is," I said, pulling it out of the drawer. It actually matched the valentines I was going to be passing out today. It had the same shark head on it.

I threw on my shirt and a pair of pants. "Now I just need some socks," I mumbled to myself, "and then I'll be all set."

I searched my sock drawer for my pair of red socks. My mom had given them to me last year on Valentine's Day. They were bright red and had sharks all over them, of course!

I looked through every pair of socks, but I couldn't find them. Then I remembered that I had worn them on Tuesday. Maybe they were still in the dirty-clothes hamper.

I dashed back to the bathroom and crashed into Suzie just as she was coming out.

"Hey! Watch it!" Suzie snapped. "What's the emergency this time? Are your pants on fire?"

"No! My pants are not on fire! I'm trying to find my red socks."

"I see you have on your red shirt, and you're looking for your red socks. Don't forget to put on your underwear with the little red hearts," Suzie said, smirking. "They are perfect for Valentine's Day."

"I don't have underwear with hearts on it!" I yelled. "Now get out of my way so I can find my socks!"

I pushed Suzie aside, ran into the bathroom, and threw open the hamper. I stuck my head in, but I didn't see my socks.

"They've got to be in here," I said to myself. I pushed some clothes around and saw a flash of red. I stuck my hand down deeper and pulled out . . . ONE red sock.

"UGH!" I groaned. "Where is the other one?"

I started throwing the dirty clothes out of the hamper, desperately searching for my other sock. I didn't realize that Suzie had walked back into the bathroom to grab her heart earrings.

"EEEWWWWW!" she screamed. "That is disgusting! A pair of your dirty underwear just hit me in the face!"

"Sorry!" I muttered. "I'm trying to find my other red sock."

Suzie growled and left the bathroom.

By now, I had thrown all of the clothes out of the hamper and still hadn't found the sock.

I threw my hands up in the air. "Great! Just great!" I said. "I'm going to have to wear only one red sock."

Just then my mom called from downstairs, "Freddy, Freddy, you need to come down and eat breakfast! The bus will be here soon!"

"Coming, Mom!" I answered. I grabbed another sock from my drawer and ran downstairs to the kitchen.

A big smile crossed my face when I got to my

seat at the table. There was a little stuffed shark holding a heart in his mouth that said, I LOVE YOU SO MUCH I COULD EAT YOU UP!

"Happy Valentine's Day!" said my mom and dad.

"Thanks," I said, picking up the stuffed shark and giving it a hug.

"Sit down, Freddy," said my mom. "I made you a special Valentine's Day breakfast."

My mom always made us something special for Valentine's Day. I couldn't wait to see what it was this year.

I sat down, and my mom brought over a plate with heart-shaped pancakes that had strawberries and whipped cream on top.

"Mmmmmmm . . . These look delicious!" I said, rubbing my tummy.

I stuck my finger in the whipped cream and licked it off. Then I poured some maple syrup on my pancakes, picked one up with my hands, and took a giant bite.

My dad looked over at me and shook his head.

"What?" I said with a mouthful of pancake.

"Do you see these?" he said, holding up his silverware. "This is called a knife, and this is called a fork. People use them to eat with."

I laughed, stabbed another piece of pancake with my fork, and shoved it into my mouth.

"Mom also made us strawberry smoothies," said Suzie.

"Really? I love strawberry smoothies!" I said, taking a sip. "So does this little shark here. He loves strawberry smoothies, too!"

I picked up the shark and pretended he was drinking the smoothie. I put his mouth around the straw. *CHOMP!*

I guess I chomped down a little too hard because the glass tipped over and pink smoothie spilled all over the table, dripped onto my pants, and made a pink puddle on the floor.

"Oops," I whispered. "Sorry, Mom."

My mom sighed. "I know it was an accident, Freddy, but these kinds of things wouldn't happen if you weren't fooling around like that."

"Sorry," I said again. My Valentine's Day was not off to a great start.

"I'll clean up this mess," said my mom. "You need to run upstairs and change your pants. You can't go to school like that."

I sprinted upstairs, put on a new pair of pants, flew back down to the kitchen, and skidded into my seat at the table.

"The bus will be here any minute," said my dad. "Eat up."

I shoveled forkfuls of pancake into my mouth. I didn't want to waste one delicious bite.

"I put your valentines in your backpack and your heart cookies in this plastic bag," said my mom. "I didn't want to put the cookies in your backpack because I don't want them to get crushed."

"Good idea! Thanks, Mom," I said. "The kids are going to love the cookies."

"Just be very careful with them," said my mom.

I gave her a thumbs-up and smiled. "I will."

Just then the bus pulled up in front of our house. "Time to go," said my dad.

I grabbed my backpack and the bag of cookies.

"Make sure you have everything," my mom called after me.

I was halfway out the door when I remembered I had forgotten something very important . . . my extra-special valentine for Miss Clark!

I ran upstairs, grabbed the valentine off my nightstand, and gently put it in my jacket pocket.

"Freddy!" my dad called from downstairs. "The bus is about to leave without you! Let's go!"

I patted my jacket pocket and grinned. Miss Clark was going to love my valentine.

I bounded down the stairs and out the door to the bus.

CHAPTER 7

Disaster!

I leaped onto the bus. "Good morning, Mr. Franklin. Happy Valentine's Day!" I said to my bus driver, and handed him one of the heart cookies I had made. "This is for you."

"Thanks, Freddy. This looks delicious. Happy Valentine's Day to you, too!" he said. "I like your two different colored socks. Is that a new style?"

I laughed. "Nope. I just couldn't find my other red one."

I started to walk to my seat. Every morning Max usually stuck his foot out into the aisle and tried to trip me. This morning I paid

extra-careful attention to where I was going because I didn't want anything to happen to the cookies I was carrying.

I kept my eyes on the ground as I made my way down the aisle. I breathed a sigh of relief when I was safely past Max's seat. "Phew!"

Then before I knew what was happening, I felt something yank me backwards. I tried to stay on my feet, but I fell down right on top of the bag of cookies.

I looked up and saw Max pointing at me and laughing hysterically. "Ha, ha, ha, ha, ha! Happy Valentine's Day, Freddy!" he said.

I pulled the bag of cookies out from under me and looked inside. They were all crushed. I wanted to cry, but I didn't want Max to call me a baby, so I slowly got up and made my way to my seat.

"Are you okay, Freddy?" Robbie asked.

"I'm fine, but the cookies Josh and I made for our class party today are all smashed," I said, sniffling and trying to hold back my tears.

"It's okay," said Josh.

"No, it's not! It's a disaster!" I said. "Just look at them." I held the bag open so Josh could look inside.

He peered inside. "Those are definitely some broken hearts."

"We worked so hard on them," I said. "Now they're ruined!"

"It's okay, Freddy," said Jessie. "I'm sure the pieces will still be tasty."

"Why did he have to do that?" I whispered

to Josh. "Max is such a bully. He's always doing mean things to kids."

Max turned around in his seat. "What did you just say?"

I gulped. "Nothing," I mumbled.

Max grabbed my shirt. "I know you said something about me."

"Let go of him, Max," said Josh.

Max twisted my shirt tighter.

"I said, let go of him," Josh repeated, grabbing Max's hand and yanking it off my shirt.

Josh was so brave. He always was an ally to his friends and stood up to Max, the biggest bully in the whole second grade.

"I'll tell you what Freddy said. He said you're a bully."

Max glared at Josh.

"Freddy and I worked really hard making cookies for our class party," said Josh, "and now because of you, they are all broken!"

Max stared at Josh for a minute, and then he sat back down in his seat.

"What are we going to do?" I said to Josh.

"We'll just tell Miss Clark what happened," said Josh. "She'll understand."

"And like Jessie said, I'm sure the cookie pieces will taste just as delicious as a whole cookie," Robbie said, trying to make me feel better.

I smiled at him and sighed. "I guess."

"Did you get all of your valentines done?" asked Robbie.

"Yep. I know you're not in my class this year, but I still made one for you," I said. I reached into my backpack and pulled out one for Robbie. "Here you go."

"Wow! These are really cool," said Robbie. "They look like the shark on the *Jaws* poster."

I took off my jacket and put it down next to me on the seat. "And look! I even have a shirt to match," I said.

All of a sudden, Max shouted, "Hey! What's that stinky smell?"

"You!" said Jessie. "You're smelling yourself."

I giggled. When it came to Max, Jessie was also really brave.

Max ignored her. "It smells like stinky perfume." He turned and pointed to Chloe. "I bet it's you. You said you were going to put perfume on your valentines."

Chloe shook her head.

Max reached across the aisle and grabbed Chloe's bag of valentines.

"Hey! Give me those back," Chloe whined.

Max put the bag of valentines up to his nose and sniffed. "I don't smell any perfume," he said.

"I changed my mind," said Chloe. "I didn't

spray any perfume on my valentines. I just put on some of those scratch-'n'-sniff stickers."

Max threw the bag of valentines back to Chloe.

"Well, I know I smell perfume," said Max. "There is perfume around here somewhere." He sniffed the air some more and looked around.

I swallowed hard and patted the valentine in my jacket pocket. Then I reached into my pocket and rubbed my lucky shark's tooth. *Don't look at me*, I thought to myself. *Don't look at me.*

Max kept sniffing the air. "Sniff . . . sniff . . . sniff . . . I know it's here somewhere," he said.

I sank down in my seat, trying to make myself invisible.

Just then Max jumped up and grabbed my jacket before I had a chance to stop him.

He put the jacket up to his nose. "Ah-ha! It's in here," he said, sticking his hand into my jacket pocket.

He pulled out the valentine I had made for Miss Clark. "Well, well, well, what do we have here?" he said, chuckling.

I lunged toward him. "Give that back!" I yelled.

Max pulled his hand out of my reach. "Isn't this sweet. Freddy made a special valentine for Miss Clark."

I lunged at Max one more time and got my hands on the valentine. "I said give it back!" I shouted.

Max held on tight and pulled harder.

RIP! The valentine ripped in half.

My mouth dropped open, and Max's eyes got wide.

I sank down in my seat and buried my head

in my hands. "No, no, no, no! Everything's ruined," I whispered.

Robbie patted me on the shoulder. "It will be okay, Freddy."

"Now look what you've done!" Josh barked.

He yanked the other half of my valentine out of Max's hand and gave it back to me. "Here you go, Freddy."

"Thanks," I mumbled.

Jessie smiled at me. "That valentine is really beautiful, Freddy. It just needs a little more glitter. Then it will be as good as new," she said.

"I know you're trying to make me feel better, but it won't be as good as new. It's ruined! This day is a total disaster, and it's only eight o'clock in the morning!"

"It's not a disaster," said Josh.

"Yes, it is!" I wailed. "I couldn't find one of my red socks. I spilled smoothie on my pants. The cookies are totally crushed, and now my extra-special valentine is ripped. What else can go wrong?"

CHAPTER 8

Mended Hearts

The bus finally arrived at school, and everyone jumped off with big smiles on their faces . . . everyone except me.

Jessie put her arm around my shoulder. "Hey, Freddy," she said. "Don't look so sad. You've got to turn that frown upside down! It's Valentine's Day. You love Valentine's Day!"

"After everything that has happened so far this morning, I'm not sure I even *like* Valentine's Day anymore," I said.

"Of course you do," said Jessie, gently poking my cheek with her finger. "Now, let me see that smile . . . Come on . . . Come on, Freddy . . . Where's that smile?"

I couldn't help but giggle, because Jessie was tickling my face.

"Oh! There it is!" said Jessie. "I knew it was in there somewhere." She grabbed my hand. "Come on, Miss Clark is waiting for us."

As soon as she said "Miss Clark," my smile turned back into a frown. I remembered the ripped valentine in my pocket and the bag of broken cookies.

Jessie dragged me down the hall to our classroom. When we got to the door, we froze and our eyes got big and wide.

"Wow!" said Jessie. "Look at this!"

"Wow! This is amazing!" I said.

Miss Clark had decorated the whole classroom. There were pink and red streamers hanging from the ceiling, heart decorations everywhere, and everyone had a red balloon tied to their chair.

"Excuse me! Excuse me!" came Chloe's voice

from behind us. "You need to move. I need to get in."

She pushed herself in between Jessie and me and ran right up to Miss Clark. "Miss Clark! Miss Clark! Look at these Jell-O hearts my nana made for our party. Aren't they beautiful?"

"They *are* beautiful, Chloe," said Miss Clark. "You will have to thank your nana for us."

Jessie bounded into the room to look at Chloe's Jell-O hearts, but I remained frozen at the doorway.

"Chloe, those are really cool," said Jessie. "I like how they jiggle."

Chloe giggled. "They're wiggly and jiggly," she said. Then she put her hands on her hips and wiggled them around.

Jessie unzipped her backpack and pulled out a big plastic bottle of bright red juice. "Here, Miss Clark," she said. "This is the *agua fresca* that my *abuela* made. It's my favorite flavor . . . watermelon!"

"This looks delicious, Jessie," said Miss Clark. "I can't wait to try it! You will also have to thank your grandmother for us."

Miss Clark loved the treats Chloe and Jessie brought in. She was going to hate our broken cookies.

Josh saw me standing there and ran over. "Come on, Freddy," said Josh. "Let's give Miss Clark our cookies."

"I don't want to," I whispered.

"What do you mean you don't want to?" asked Josh.

Miss Clark saw us standing in the doorway and came over. "Is everything okay, boys?" she asked.

I hung my head and stared at the floor.

"Freddy, what's wrong?" asked Miss Clark. "I thought you loved Valentine's Day."

"I used to," I mumbled.

"You used to?" Miss Clark chuckled. "But you don't anymore?"

"No, not anymore," I muttered.

"Why not?" asked Miss Clark.

I let out a big sigh. "Because it's a disaster! A total disaster!"

Miss Clark smiled. "What do you mean?" she asked. "It's only eight o'clock in the morning. It can't be that much of a disaster."

I sniffled. "But it is! Just look," I said, holding up the bag of broken cookies.

"What's this?" Miss Clark asked, looking inside the bag.

"It was supposed to be our cookies for the party, but they're ruined!"

"What happened?" said Miss Clark.

"Max," I said, pointing in his direction. "That's what happened."

Miss Clark stared at me with a puzzled look on her face.

"Max tripped Freddy on the bus this morning," said Josh, "and Freddy fell on the cookies."

"Oh my goodness!" said Miss Clark. "I'm so sorry that happened to you, Freddy. That's terrible!"

"It *is* terrible!" I said. "Josh and I worked so hard making them. I wanted them to be perfect." I sniffled.

"But they *are* perfect," said Miss Clark.

Now it was my turn to look confused. "No, they're not," I mumbled.

"Well, I love them," said Miss Clark. "I'm going to call them broken heart cookies, and during our party, it will be everyone's job to mend a broken heart."

"Huh?"

"Everyone will get some cookie pieces," said Miss Clark, "and they can put them back together, just like a puzzle, to make a whole heart."

"I like that idea," said Jessie. "No one should have a broken heart on Valentine's Day, and we can all fix that!"

"Exactly!" said Miss Clark.

"See, Freddy," whispered Josh. "I told you it wasn't a total disaster."

I handed Miss Clark the bag of cookies, and she went to go put them down in the back of the room.

"Ummm . . . I think you're forgetting something," I whispered to Josh.

"Now what?" said Josh.

I silently pointed to my jacket pocket.

Josh just stared at me.

I carefully pulled my ripped valentine out of my pocket and turned my back to Miss Clark so she couldn't see it. "What am I supposed to do about this?"

"Oh, that's no big deal, Freddy," said Josh.

"Maybe not to you," I said. "But it is to me."

"No, I just meant that that's easy to fix," said Josh. "You stay here. I'll go get some tape."

While everyone was busy putting their things away, Josh went over to the shelf and grabbed the tape. "Here you go, Freddy," he whispered.

"Thanks," I said. I laid the two pieces of the valentine down on a table and carefully matched them up. Then I taped them together and held up the valentine.

"See?" said Josh. "Good as new!"

"Do you really think so?" I asked.

Josh nodded and gave me a little push in Miss Clark's direction. "Go give it to her."

I hid the valentine behind my back and walked over to Miss Clark. I was a little nervous. I could feel my heart beating in my chest.

"Ummm . . . Miss Clark . . . I have something for you," I said.

Miss Clark smiled. "But you already gave me the cookies, Freddy," she said.

"I have something else. Here," I said, handing her the valentine.

Miss Clark just stood there looking at the valentine, not saying a word. *Oh no!* I thought to myself. *She hates it.*

Then a huge smile spread across her face. "Oh, Freddy! I love it!" she said, giving me a great big hug. "It's the most beautiful valentine I have ever gotten!"

I smiled. Maybe this Valentine's Day wasn't such a disaster after all!

Freddy's Fun Pages

WATERMELON AGUA FRESCA

If you would like to try the watermelon *agua fresca* that Jessie brought to school for the Valentine's Day party, then you can make it using this recipe! Be sure to ask an adult for help with the cutting and blending!

Ingredients:

4 cups cubed, seeded watermelon

½ cup water

¼ cup white sugar

2 tablespoons lime juice

Directions:

1. Make sure the watermelon is cut into small cubes with the seeds removed.

2. Put the watermelon, water, and sugar in a blender and puree until smooth.

3. Add the lime juice and blend for another few seconds.

4. Pour the drink into a large pitcher and refrigerate until well chilled.

5. Share with your friends and family.

Enjoy!

CANDY HEARTS BOAT CHALLENGE

Try this fun Valentine STEM challenge with your friends and family!
Using a 4 x 4-inch square of foil, create a boat that holds the most candy hearts.

Materials:

1. Plastic tub filled with water
2. Aluminum foil
3. Scissors
4. Ruler
5. Candy hearts

Directions:

1. Measure and cut a square of aluminum foil that is 4 x 4 inches.
2. Using just the piece of foil, design and create a boat that will hold candy hearts.

3. Place your boat in the tub of water.

4. Gently place candy hearts into your boat one at a time, counting them as you go.

5. Continue placing candy hearts in your boat until it starts to sink!

6. The winner is the person whose boat can hold the most hearts!

Good luck!

VALENTINE'S GAME CHALLENGE!

Have some fun on Valentine's Day like Freddy and his friends with these awesome games for home or school!

Candy in the Bowl

1. Place some wrapped valentine candy in a bowl.

2. Put on a pair of mittens.

3. Take one piece of candy out of the bowl and try to unwrap it with your mittens on!

4. The person who can unwrap their candy first is the winner!

Heart Relay

1. Put candy hearts in a bowl.

2. Pick up one candy heart using chopsticks.

3. Carry the candy heart across the room using your chopsticks.

4. If it drops, you have to go back to the beginning and start over!

5. The first person to make it across the room and back without dropping the candy heart is the winner!

Special Delivery

1. Make a paper airplane.

2. Throw your airplane at a heart-shaped target that is lying on the floor across the room from you.

3. The person whose airplane lands closest to the target is the winner!

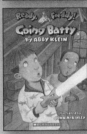